# APHRODITE'S
# GLEAMING PEARLS

### POETRY & PROSE
### EVELYN CHARLES

First edition July 2024

Cover Illustration by Evelyn Charles

Print First Edition ISBN: 978-1-0689238-0-7
ebook First Edition ISBN: 978-1-0689238-1-4

*To my dearest love*

# Table of Contents

## Ode to Aphrodite

Aphrodite carved herself
from Sea's crashing waves

into a goddess,
luminous of love and lust,

embracing the world with her body,
altering the tides with her light.

Evelyn Charles

*Soft as water flows,*
*your lips linger on my skin.*

## The Beauty of Pleasure

Waves on the wine dark sea
are a force upon the shivering surface,
building steady, a rising rhythm with crests
of aqua spirals reaching into the sun,
until, brimming with height,
their glistening iridescence
trembles along the shoreline,

painting the sand with an airy
coating of sea foam, rich of
Aphrodite's gleaming pearls,

rising and
falling
on the body

In as ample abundance
as slivers of sunlight,

speckled on the earth.

## *Along Aphrodite's Shores*

I stretch my limbs on the sand,
embracing the hot touch
of the sun's constant gaze,

I welcome the heat –
enveloped in the sighs of the wind
and the roars of the waters,

in the times of gods,
Lovers paced these beaches
desperate to swim across the waves

where I float in the shallows,
dragging my feet along the ripples,
all is languid as you pull me into your currents,

there is a sun of our own between us,
laughter bouncing in our ribs,
salt and sweetness resting on our shoulders,
we toss ourselves into the ocean's arms,
loving each other along Aphrodite's shores.

## *Yearning*

Your curls, Adonis,
they call to me,

allow me to twirl my fingers in them –
to rest my palm to your cheek,

shift your gaze, Adonis,
how soft the look of love,

when the light and shadow
kiss your features;

I would kiss them too,
should you ask me.

## Breathing

Grasping my lungs with shaking hands,
Aphrodite passes breath –
back and forth,
from the wind to my chest,
from the sands to the sea,
the shivers upon my skin
as fires stoked and teased.
Her lips graze my lips
and all at once –
I am made of air and
I cannot breathe.

## Siren Lures

My pulse hovers with eyes clenched,
thoughts tucked between fingers,
secret tales traced on my skin,

this racing heart of my body
beckons flaring visions:
*shoulders, arms, and hands,*
*fresh figs – sweet and potent,*
*smooth against hungry lips,*
*lips tasting my stomach,*
*my breasts, my neck,*

flaring heat enflamed by
the sea's silk engraved curves,
aching for attentive stares,
longing for such decadent siren lures.

## *Sustenance*

Nectar – ichor of the gods,
the golden substance that
blooms poppies, blossoms immortality,
how parched I was before you, and now,
insatiable as Aphrodite's kylix,
there is no sustenance I need
beyond drinking in your kiss.

# The Tides Sing

Aphrodite pets her golden hair,
stirs the tides within her chest,

The loose sand along the shore
is as pure as the silver in her eyes,

Amongst joyous music, kylixes overflow,
the xiphos is too heavy to lift,

She shares no sense of how
she ignites me more than bronze,
sways me more than wine,

I drink her laughter where it floats –
I would drink her words in heavy gulps,
If only she would sing to me.

## The Fire of Longing

Bring me to where they press the olives,
so I can slink against the gnarling trees,
lay in the sun and soak in the grass –
where I can groan
when my longing is drowning my senses,

with ache as oil, swelling in my throat,
The sun blazes my skin hot,
but it is not your touch,

The wind grazes my hair silk,
but it is not your touch,

Every bird claims their song
as pollen dances across the sunlight,
fragrance of flowers and fruits ripened
fall as heavy on my nose
as the rocks, sitting on earthen floor,
press into my body,

It overwhelms me
and yet
is tormentingly lacking,

Will you unleash yourself?
Slay me where I stand?
End my misery?

Aphrodite sent warnings of my desire –
promises from prophets
that I would descend the cliffs
in one of two forms:

To crumble and disperse into the earth
until there is nothing potent of my soul left
Or be condensed and woven tightly into your embrace
until the ache is so powerful it bursts, and
everything I am is fire.

## Eruption

The earth pulses between Aphrodite's hands,
its thickened water flowing hot beneath her kiss,
as steam rising from the ocean,
heat eruption is blooming power,
knowing Aphrodite's bliss.

## *Sublime*

You must be Aphrodite herself,
playful with my mortal spirit,
shifting form between beauty and allure,

a moment – a nymph,
who seeks home with the wild and vines,
another – a philosopher king,
who rules the polis soaked in wit and wine,

You must be Aphrodite herself,
as though nature were confined to a body,

meeting with you is
drawing invitations for the stars
to grace my open palms,

Having you is the cliffs,
shifting their winds,
to lay amongst my humble grove of trees.

## Lyre

He wields the music of his body,
with drawn out movements
that invoke Apollo's hazy shimmer –
A vibration of strings hung in the air,
A hum when he strums me like his lyre,
A prophecy brushed on my lips,
my lips, ajar, by the music of his love.

## Alluring Tides

When all in sight is endless waves,
I understand the traveler's tales,
those windblown cautions
shaken from the water's surface
begin their rhythmic motion
on shores edge:

*Oh, how sailors dive willingly into the deep,*
*never to surface,*
*Golden gifts,*
*Amphorae filled to brim,*
*Oils and wines,*
*left to line the darkest of depths*
*amongst shattered wooden boards*

the men lounge
with clean hands and dry tunics
scoffing at the fools,
of those whose longing for pleasure
tossed them over bows edge.
The men roar with laughter,
as their cups spill dark wine.

The sea reflects the light
as morning approaches,
it holds my breath, my gaze,
and begins to whisper in my mind:

*Oh, how sirens dive willingly into the deep,*
*seldom to regret,*
*Luminous skin,*
*Charmed songs on lush lips,*
*Corals and shine,*
*abundant in riches of the ocean's breadth*
*inviting you to taste its supple hoards*

I approach, against wisdom,
wading into your alluring tides,
I am the Hesperian dragon,
drawn to the gravity of your golden heart,
I am Charybdis,
insatiable for all I desire,
I am the ever, clever Odysseus,
whose wit cannot quell their lust,

I sink into the sea of your arms,
swim in the depths of your touch.

## *Wrapped in Waves*

The curve and bend of his back
are waves of his body,
the grooves of muscle
are an anchor,
steadying me over tides I cannot surface,

the engulfing pleasure
both drowns and lifts my breath

with his arms wrapped around me –
can he feel how I soften in his embrace?

## *Devotion*

Aphrodite, the smiling lynx, led me,
an unfaithful believer
whose cup's libations lay dry,
wandering up the protruding cliffs
where waves tease their melody,
salt sprays my skin, and vines
stretch up my thighs,

I climbed with burning lungs
until I came across your path
and dared to question
if I had breached Olympus,

for you – golden haired and luminous,
must have been shaped of divine sea and sky

with a peplos of Athena's craft
and a smile akin to Hestia's hearth,
your graceful movements toward me,
subtle poppies scent of the earth,

and when you lift your shining eyes,
casting your stare to mine,
I plead with Aphrodite,
I have known devotion ever since.

## *Hope*

What an arrow –
The day that bursts into orange
beneath a sky, striking an effortless sigh
into waves and wind

What a trickster –
That god who leads you here,
to the sands where I lay
painted in the glow of my frame

What a jar –
That slips from your grasp,
so enchantingly sculpted and painted,
with wings of your gasp
when our eyes meet by chance,
to roll and tip over,
pouring into my breath
the hope that Pandora always craved.

# The Heart of Icarus

Eros crafts wings of melted wax
with drips of desire
sinking into sea salt spray,

the gods watch, layered in bronze feathers,
intrigued by the teasing flames
that lick and ignite the sculpted heart,
a flurry of shapes, engulfed in heat,
soaring into the turbulent waves.

Eros, the wise and foolish,
weeps in mourning:

he will never know the pleasure
of being consumed by the scorching sun.

*Aphrodite scolds my hubris,*
*though it is she who blesses me with it.*

## *Godhood*

Your body to my body
ascends me to godhood,
the depths of the oceans,
the closeness of the shallows,
are Aphrodite's strength and weakness
wrapped in my trembling sighs.

## Whirlpool

Exposed collar bones,
shadows hung
on rippling curves,
hands clung
to the waves of your skin,

shifting shimmer,
encompassing tide,
your embrace is a swirling current
past the glaze of the sea's surface
drawing me deeper in,

how sweet your lips to sink into,
tasting the salt of the depths of touch,
grasping your hips and swaying together
is the music of the whirlpool –
Aphrodite's motion, her flooding rush.

## *Lengthen Out to Sea*

The muses lengthen out to sea
with an ache to reach the tide,
my body pulses when you near me,
yearning for floods to rise.

## Tasting Aphrodite's Waters

She has a hero's body
when she unearths me on the beach.

For eons, the gods would visit where I lay,
deep in the sand, longing for the lapping waves
while the shores encrusted around my form,

A beautiful wasteland, adorned
in the glaze of earthen jewels,
opulent with buried hope,
teased by turquoise water,
Aphrodite's sea hidden beyond reach.

She lifts me from the shoreline –
austere, as she shakes me free
from the satin shine of sand,

she kisses my pearl crested collarbones,
my shell coated torso,
shows me the steadiness of my feet
and guides me, hand in hand,
to taste Aphrodite's waters.

## *Loom*

Knead your fingers in my hair
as I wrap mine across your thighs

we are the rivers, turquoise waters
swirling like threads

stretched upon your loom,
the wool soaked in saffron dye –

honey dyes, dripping from my lips,
my eyes seek you beneath panting breaths,

caress my cheek, my chin,
I am both unraveled and woven
in your hand.

## Joy of Aphrodite

I shudder when you touch me,
enticed by the delight in your eyes,
you seek the joy of Aphrodite –
being the cause of my pleasure.

## *Drawn to You*

Swayed by currents
as Dawn erupts in orange shades each morning,

pulled by power
as strongly as the god's oaths press on the mind,

led by inevitability
as all the stars lay scattered around the moon
yet appear each darkened night,

I am drawn to you,
with frenzied soul,

facing this ceaseless nature of desire
until my hands are woven threads of fate,
mended to your touch.

# *Enveloped*

It is like the bath.

Its waters embracing me,
every fragment of my body,
each nook of my fingers,
endless crevices of my limbs
explored and held,

It is like the ocean.

The waves pushing and pulling
with an overwhelming force
of rising tides and lingering pressure,

It is like the volcano.

that searing touch of growing heat,
tension of the rocks,
aching and brimming,
from below the surface
until the limbs of the earth
shake with rising flames
that become all encompassing,

It is unlike anything I know –

being with your heart,
I am enveloped by you.

## *Firing Clay*

Stumbling with you in the dark
is pure intoxication,
wines and incense,
bliss and extravagance,
which could never entice me as fully
as the velvet of your kiss,

loving you in the dark
is learning the song of your skin,
clinging to your voice
rising in rhythm,
every decision, every choice,
aimed at savouring the music of your touch

holding you in the dark
is the sculpting of clay,
pressed into precise forms –
the grandest of kraters,
the finest of kylixes,
your body molding into my hands,
our unity fired
with the rise of the morning sun.

## *Muse*

Trace me with your tongue
and rest your cheeks against my thighs,
allow my touch, tender upon your gentle head,
to entangle through your hair,
swaying my hips into your kiss,
your kiss – the muse of my sighs.

## *Amplify*

Desire and fire
make home in
my abdomen

when my eyes, seizing where
my fingertips can trace
the curve of your neck,
feast on every freckle,
every constellation of your frame,

I crave to learn
your body as
my homeland:

to burn the memory
of your movements, your smile,
against the shape of the shoreline,
as if overlaid into me,
drinking the waters of Eros in eager gulps,
to pray for sight in darkness,
taste in starvation,
touch in the desert,

To embrace
and amplify
my senses

So, when pleasure leaps with gasps,
my writhing limbs, my arching back,
when my senses are overwhelmed
past recognition –
I miss not even a moment of knowing you.

## A Golden Tapestry

We laugh into each other's arms,
laying upon the tree's humble earth,
with your eyes as fluttering as the swallows
that play through the wind,
all that we say erupts delight between us

Twirling the strands of my hair between your fingers,
you are as devoted as Penelope before her loom,
claiming my stories are more intricate
than any of the great epics,

Ease floats across the sky
until horizon has met horizon
and still, we lay, our bodies
knotted together like threads

you muse how we should journey home
before the night's weight sinks,
I plan how I could weave a life full of days with you.

## Adorning Love

Your touch forms pearls
woven through my hair,
rubies that speckle my skin,
your Midas heart caresses my bones:
casts the fragrance of lilies
soaked in my touch,
blossoming sapphire of my eyes,
lathering my laughter in silver dust,
Aphrodite lays me in the shallows
of the vibrant, glistening waters,
I am opulence,
I am splendour,
your adorning kiss sends my spirit
golden to Olympus above,
I am Love –
I am loved.

## *The Sea's Nature*

The wind off the coast carries air like sweat,
heavy with salt,
as prominent as the sun.

The house of Poseidon is a temple,
rising above jagged rocks,
sharing his nature – with waves
that extend their longing,
crashing upon marble halls,

such force, the pressure,
of waves on stone, of his body to my body,
strong against the cool touch of the column,
and yet, his hand –
cupped to the round of my head,
is the lightness of seafoam, gentle in the shallows,

Here,
where the winds toss our kisses
as grains of sand,
Aphrodite's song
is humming on the rays of sunlight,

we are breathless of misted spray
reaching cresting waves,
soothed against the jagged rocks,
rising in Poseidon's kingdom.

## My Pleasure is Yours

Wrap my needs into your hands,
hold my pleasure in your gaze,
it belongs there with you.

# Divinity

I grasp you,
caress you,
as dearly as I would
clutch a rhyton
pouring libations to the gods.

*Would you make me your goddess?*

Pampering my skin with the kiss
of your prayers,
massaging oil into the nook
between my shoulder blades
as your performed sacred rites,

*Am I your goddess?*

When your lips are gentle
upon the tops of my feet,
while you kneel
before my smiling beauty
with my hands, light upon your head
and my thumb, tucked into your kiss,

As I grasp you,
caress you,
would you honour me with libations?
would you spill yourself for me?

## *Sweetness*

I have developed a taste for your sweetness,

No rain will cleanse me,
No sea will wash me,

There is no hope for the serpent
once it is hooked on nectar.

## *Desire*

I sit beneath the stars
unsure of how the moon
shines with such power

Whispering, I ask,
*What is the force that pulls and draws the waves?*

The moon hums and gleams
with glowing pulses

*My silver fire*
*that paints the earth*
*is desire*

Oh,

Desire,

What a supple word
to indulge upon the tongue –

*Desire*

As I taste the starlit wine,
drunk on my body's motion in the sand,
I stir in her silver light,

Tugging at my heart,
pulling sensual stretches of my limbs,
my body is as the water
beneath the full moon,
inhaling starlight, exhaling love –
swayed by desire.

## *Sensational Depths*

A cooling pool of crystal waters,
twinkling with ripples,
flutters around the submerged Aphrodite,

as she breaths,
her chest rises
and falls,
her hips roll
in the lapping reflections,
her own fingers press
lightly on her breasts,

her stare swallows me
as the cooling pool
grows into oceans,
warm and engulfing,
with corals shining
as stars of another realm,
where I am tossed beneath the depths
into foreign sensation
and honoured as her guest.

## Lyrics of Love

Those sultry words lay hot on my ears,
fall lost on my laboured breathing,

Your body is the weight of the sky,
blanketed on the sea,

Every grain of sand could not shine me
as iridescent as your voice.

## *Creation in Your Hands*

You hold me with such grip,
such cautious desperation,

as if I am Oceanus – writhing and slipping
from your grasp, as though your world
is dependent on the hold you have on my body,

you hold me with such love,
such frantic admiration,

it is as being the earthen clay,
clasped by tender hands,
held with beaming awe,
as though my shape, my soul,
my body you hold,
is the beauty of first creation.

## Irises Blossom

Irises blossom across the garden's pond,
the columns of the temples,
sculpted in arching lines,
hold the high sun's cascading warmth,

Immersed in the marble
live delicate scenes
painted brightly of spring's eruption –
hush blues budding, birds nibbling,
swans floating upon the streams,

I am a witness of artistry:
the flowers, abundant in the summer air,
grace the grounds with vibrance,
their colour and scents
form the temple
into a pulsing place of power
where Aphrodite's languid presence
is overwhelming to my limbs,

Here where I lay,
the flow of my dress
Brushing upon my hips,
my hair, free and flying,
In the reflections of the temple's pools,

I am a nymph,

As one of the plants and trees
entangled with the earth and sky,

I am a flower,

As rich with sunshine as any golden petal,

I am a woman,

Whose body is home of light, life, and love.

## In the Sea Together

Smashed against the rocks,
the waves break through
with crashing force –

I roll your body as a ship,
the great trireme
tossed in Poseidon's grip.

Do you enjoy me here?
Over you, as Olympus,
embedding my heart as starry Asteria
whose islands cliffs rise
protruding from the ocean's depths,
with my hands locked to your hands,
with my hips on lulling waves,
maneuvering our bodies as the sea.

Evelyn Charles

*I have died of pleasure in your arms,*
*Resurrect me.*

## Star in the Distance

The purest stardust lives as sea foam
rising on the crests of waves,
golden ichor glistening in the sun,
reaching outstretched until
pulled to the shore and
kissed across the sand,

I long to ascend to such horizons –
lift me to the stars
while holding me close to your chest

the strength of the waves is your arms,
the muscles of your back,
transform my body
to the ocean's weightless peak,
lest I become a star in the distance,
pull me deeper to you.

## Insatiable Touch

The sea's water coats my thighs
the way your hands do –
hungrily lapping the smooth skin
where fabric does not touch.

# A Prismatic Tapestry

My days become woven:
oil lights, braided hair,
low hanging orange trees,
your thumb rubbing
against the back of my hand,
warm winds, sunset glow,
freshly baked bread,
lyrical laughter, coaxing waves,
shells that gleam beneath the day,
steady embraces, quiet breaths,
evenings where I watch
the rise and fall of your chest,
words of oaths recited
in daily promise whispered
on gentle lips, your lips,
a tapestry of kisses,
my neck, my forehead,
brow to brow –
we rest there together.

## Flush

Aphrodite's kisses are a stain on my lips,
A tint on my cheeks,
A memory in my mind
that blesses me forever flush.

# The Sun Beckons Spring

The birds' songs flood the air
just as the songs
that escape my lungs
while wrapped with you
in early morning.

The bright promise of spring
hangs on the wind, on our breath,
an anticipation:

of Persephone embracing her mother,
of nymphs weaving crowns of petals,
of entangled limbs and sunbathed days
where my head rests on your chest on meadow floor,

the earth stretches as I do –
with release of tension in great breath,
she is on edge just as we are,
with shaking limbs and pounding hearts

ready for all to blossom.

## *Pleasure*

Pearls form in the delicate space
between your lips,
where your tongue sculpts
divine epithets of your kiss,
their iridescence and mythic beauty
gleams from the power of your love.

## *Incantations*

Tossing your name
between my lips
to taste its vibration,

the shape of my tongue
twists and lingers
on promises of devotion,

I am a mouthpiece
of the gods,
bowing to my words,

our whispers together
seals the oath
into each other's kiss:

*I love you*

## *The Sculptor*

Make a statue of me:

sculpt me with your hands,
press the details with your fingertips,
your tongue, your kiss,

capture what it is
of my face, of my body,
that inspires you to see me as beautiful.

perhaps then, when I still feel
the shades of mist of your hands on me,
gazing in bronze reflection,
I will see beauty too.

# The Eternal Glow of Dusk

While the sun is low,
orange kisses your frame,
painting the world into Elysium,
those hanging gardens that hover
with floating flowers are
as intricate as your eyes,

while the sun is low,
citrus bursts on my tongue
as potent as promises,
in the space before the night will break,
you are the licking flames of godhood
shining before me,

while the sun is low,
swaying together is blazing as Helios,
every breath on my skin
is sacred fire,
your love floods my veins
with endless glow,
nearing you is knowing the sun,
while the sun is low.

## *Beneath Your Steady Hands*

Your fingers gently glide
with the oils of Eros
drawing forth weakened sighs –
eyes that softly close.

## Golden

Your patience draws
the iris flowers to raise their petals,
embracing their reflection
in the surface below,

soaring birds
bow their wings to your gentle words,
in earnest, to share in your conversation,

the waves themselves
soften in their shimmer,
in presence of your tender nature,

you, beautiful as sunlight,
ensnare my attention,
my gaze is on your spirit –
the muses painting vividly
your golden shade.

## *Swaying*

Your heartbeat shares
the shade of moon light –
it draws me forward,
as though I were the tide,
the waters that lean into your song.

Sing to me,
Pull me closer.

## Washing Stars Across Sand

the gods sing when the night washes
the stars across the sands,
their light is a beacon
on the array of shells,
the stirring life that swells
in the shoreline's abundance

the moon's voice cascades
along the frame of your lips,
her celestial chimes echo off your touch,

every shifting of high and low tide
brings forward an empty beach,
grey against your absence,

until Aphrodite's Sea lifts your chin,
aims your gaze to mine,
and the goddess herself spills from the look

I am flooded and barren –
All my love lives in you.

Evelyn Charles

# The Thrill of Love

With my feet curled behind your neck,
love passes between us
in each desperate kiss,
these sighs, against your lips,
lift into the heavens
where Hera's oaths
and Aphrodite's pleasure
dances amongst clouds of
sparkling silk and braided crowns,
closer we are, the more my sight seeks,
reflections of my own devotion,
the thrill of the love, beaming between us.

# Lily of Knossos

The feathered woman visits me,
beaming as pure as sunlight
painted on marble stone,
she lifts her chiton through the waves,
each ankle kissing the tide,
her laughter drapes across her shoulders,
with earnest, golden smiles,

while she glides towards me
with inquiring coos,
I am fluttered with shame
of the grime and sweat on my limbs –
eager to shield away
the mishappen features of my face

My throaty heart unveils itself –

*She is a white sand lily of Knossos,*
*A daughter of the Dawn and Dove,*
*Her timeless, blooming beauty*
*Echoes my own longing for grace and love,*

though my sorrows are a song,
as brittle as driftwood,
that fall shallow in tides
which carry blood tipped spears,
she opens her wings and envelopes
my hobbling mortal frame

tending to my body
with gentle feather strokes
bathing me in goat's milk,
her dove song lingers
long after her return to sea,

I hear her sea song chimes
when I carry myself,
striding from dawn to dusk,
granting myself the same tenderness,
she once gifted me.

## Sacred Name

I sink into your kiss,
Aphrodite's name
passed between sighs
of lips on lips

*Ease*

What harmonious worship
your touch is,
trailing devotion along my spine,

enjoying our silence, presence,
together with the sun-kissed moon,

what harmonious worship
our love is,
to know peace
that does not involve sacrifice.

## An Immortal Love

Kiss, and linger,
that is what you ask of me.

In stillness,
while the sky heavies its shades,

No motion. No libations.
There were times the earth
held the sky in her palm,
ages where the sky danced
in spirals for the wind,
pressed on Atlas' brow,

you hold every constellation in your chest,
yet, kiss, and linger, is all you ask.

## Rest with me at Dawn

I hear the swans crash into the water,
the breath of their wings
collide with the wind,
they shall lift
as the arch of my back –
I connect with you
where the Dusk and Dawn mend.

*You are the essence,*
*of how love commands such great power*

Evelyn Charles

## The Shape of Aphrodite

Aphrodite smiles, sighing with her body,
as she gazes at us

Humans, all entangled together, how we fit
with the stomach pressed to the back,

legs molded to each other's legs,
the head curled into the pulse of the neck, and arms –

how sweetly the arms – wrap around and embrace
the body, with hands perfectly intertwined,

Aphrodite flutters her lashes, resting her gaze
upon the myriad of shapes we form to know her.

## Heartbeat of the Moon

Asleep, with your ear to my breast,
stirring in my embrace,
my heartbeat sings the lullaby of the earth,
is as constant a love
as the moon guided waves.

Evelyn Charles

## *Embracing the Senses*

The pearls press cool on her skin,
tight along the neck,
in lines that Aphrodite twists as chords
to the senses:

A breath of violet's scent,
the soft breeze that drags
chiton's folds against her breasts,
the chimes of Serene's stars,
her lover's steady breaths,

to know Aphrodite is to know life
as it is slowly traced along each limb –
to lead with touch,
to taste the earth,
to hear love when it sings.

## *Starlight Kisses*

The sky's brilliance
is held on the ocean's wine dark waters,
as though Aphrodite beckons Serene's light,

each star paints their forms
on the embracing still surface,
your tongue follows along the lines –
celestial clusters on my hips,

you compare the beauty of my pleasure to above,
shining as the skies,
in your embrace, I see my love,
shining in your eyes.

## *Aphrodite's Favour*

You hold Aphrodite's favour, you must,
with hair falling gently
down to shoulder's widths,
shoulders – slight and soft
as your lips, curved and pressed
olives into oil, golden life of the sun,
its shadows caught on the nape of your neck,

You hold Aphrodite's favour, your thoughts
trickling into words
as the waters cascading flow,
with eyes wielding warmth,
reaching arms, open of hope,
the strength in your body
bested only by the strength of your heart,
all you craft with clever wisdom
and nimble hands
shares traces of your light,

your motion, dancing through the shores,
your loom, coated in brittle wool
transformed into beauty
through your attention,
just as all the world in your view,

your head, light upon my chest,
your mind, dreaming in a peaceful mist,
I hold Aphrodite's favour; I hold you.